Worm Gets a Job

Kathy Caple

CANDLEWICK PRESS
CAMBRIDGE, MASSACHUSETTS

GRIMES PUBLIC LIBRARY

Al's Art Store

For Walter

First edition 2004

Library of Congress Cataloging-in-Publication Data

Caple, Kathy.
Worm gets a job / Kathy Caple. —1st ed.
p. cm.
Summary: Worm attempts various jobs for his animal friends so that
he can buy painting supplies and enter the art contest.
ISBN 0-7636-1694-X
[1. Painting—Fiction. 2. Contests—Fiction. 3. Moneymaking projects—Fiction.
4. Worms—Fiction. 5. Animals—Fiction. 6. Cartoons and comics.] I. Title.
PZ7.C17368 Wn 2004
[E]—dc21   2002025989

2 4 6 8 10 9 7 5 3 1

Printed in Singapore

This book was typeset in Stone Sans.
The illustrations were done in watercolor.

Candlewick Press
2067 Massachusetts Avenue
Cambridge, Massachusetts 02140

visit us at www.candlewick.com

Suddenly, it hit him.

Worm pushed the buggy
toward the park.

When they reached the top, Worm stopped to rest.

Finally Junior stopped crying.

But then the buggy slipped.

Worm caught the buggy and held on.

Worm headed straight to Rat's house.

Worm knocked on Stinky's door.

Worm looked at Stinky's bedroom.

Next, Worm tackled the living room.

Worm vacuumed up a sock. He vacuumed up a banana peel.

He vacuumed up a handkerchief and an old sandwich.

Just then, Stinky walked in with Aunt Fussy.

Turtle scooted by on his newspaper route.

Worm stopped at the first house and tossed the paper.

He went to the second house and tossed the paper.

He went to the third house and tossed the paper.

He went to Turtle's house and tossed the paper. . . .

Worm's customers were ready to toss *him*.

Worm stopped at Frog's Fruit Stand.

Worm went to see Frog.

Frog showed Worm his work area.

Worm got right to work.
He painted the first sign.

He painted the next sign.

Worm painted and painted. He threw himself into his work.

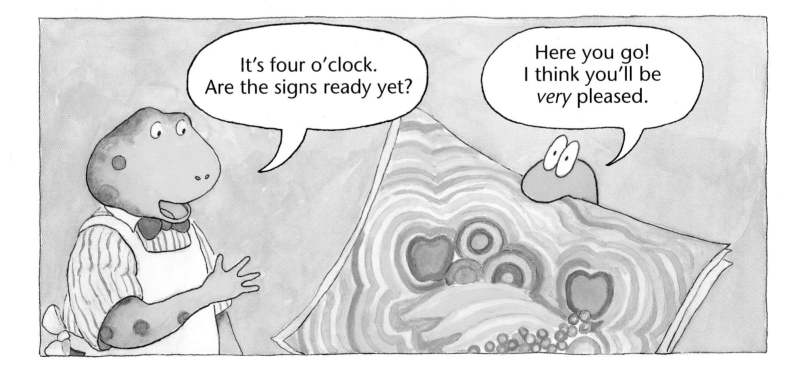

Worm was called up to accept his award.

When he got home, Worm painted and painted.

Then he had an idea.